"Growing Up Happy"
DEBRA DOESN'T TAKE THE DARE

An Emotional Literacy Book

Written by
Lawrence E. Shapiro, Ph.D.
and Illustrated by
Steve Harpster

Debra Doesn't Take the Dare
Copyright 2004, Courage to Change, LLC

Author: Lawrence E. Shapiro, Ph.D.
Illustrator: Steve Harpster

Printed in China

Summary: This book teaches children to resist peer pressure.
It also teaches children about the danger of experimenting
with alcohol.

ISBN 0-9747789-3-1

Published by:
CTC Publishing
A Division of Courage to Change
10400 Eaton Place, Suite 140
Fairfax, Virginia 22030
703-383-3075
Fax: 703-383-3076
Web Site: www.couragetochange.com

For special discounts on volume orders, please call 703-383-3075.

Dear Boys and Girls,

Did anyone ever dare you to do something that you knew was wrong? Were you able to say 'no,' or did you do something that you shouldn't have?

Everyone wants to be popular and well-liked, and this sometimes makes kids (and even adults) do things that they shouldn't.

This book is about a girl named Debra who wants to join a club of popular girls at her school. But they want her to do something that she knows is wrong, take a drink of beer! Debra knows that children shouldn't drink beer, but she also really wants to be in the club. She is faced with a very tough decision.

When you read this book, I hope that you will learn some things you can do if other children dare you to do things that you know are wrong or unsafe. It can be very hard to do things that may get you teased or ignored by your friends, but you must always try and do the things that you know are right. Parents, teachers, and even older brothers and sisters can help. Make sure that you talk about the things that bother you, and the problems that you are facing with your friends.

Learning to make the right decision is an important part of growing up. I know that you will try hard and do your best.

Your Friend,

Dr. Larry

The phone rang on Saturday morning at exactly 10 am.

That was the time when Debra's mother said that she was allowed to have phone calls.

Debra ran to the phone and, as she expected, it was Maggie on the line.

3

"It's all set," Maggie said excitedly. "All the girls are coming over at 3 o'clock today. Did your Mom say it was okay?"

"Yeah," Debra said, "I just have to be back by dinner time."

Debra could hardly believe that she had been invited to the famous Fairmont Elementary School Cool Girls Club. Maggie had started the club over the summer and only the popular girls were invited to be members.

"Who is going to be there?" Debra asked, "Are Annie and Bethany coming?"

"Of course!" Maggie said a little too loudly, "and Darlene and Heather and Grace. And you and I make six and seven. There are only seven girls allowed in the Club, because seven is a lucky number."

"I know," Debra said, but she really wasn't sure why seven was a lucky number. She was thinking about Katie who had been number seven until about two weeks ago. Then Maggie threw Katie out of the club and Debra was invited to join. Debra wondered why Katie had been asked to leave the club. She felt a little badly, but she was also glad that there was now a place for her.

Debra hung up the phone and picked up the book that she had been reading before Maggie called. Debra loved to read and she loved to learn. Her teacher said that she was one of the best students in the class, which made Debra feel proud of herself.

But although Debra liked being smart and getting good grades, she wanted something else. Debra wanted to be popular like Maggie.

All of the girls wanted to play with Maggie during recess. All of the girls wanted to be invited over to Maggie's house on the weekends. All of the girls wanted to be in the Fairmont Elementary School Cool Girls Club that Maggie had started last summer.

And now Debra was going to be in it!

9

Even though Debra admired Maggie for being so popular, she also knew that Maggie sometimes got into trouble at school. Maggie often forgot to bring in her homework. Sometimes she was mean and bossy to other children. One time she pushed a boy down on the ground and he scraped his knee so badly he had to go to the nurse's office.

A few times Maggie talked back to their teacher, and that really meant trouble! Maggie was sent to the Principal's office and her parents had to come in for a conference.

PRINCIPAL

When Maggie got in trouble for making faces she told Debra, "I don't care what the teacher says. She doesn't know everything."

Debra knew that Maggie's behavior was wrong, but she liked her anyway. She wasn't really sure why.

I think that it is always important to treat other people nicely and have good behavior. What do you think?

Debra arrived at Maggie's house at three o'clock on the button. She didn't want to be late and she didn't want to be early either. Maggie and the other five girls were already there and Maggie's mother led Debra to the basement.

When Debra came down the stairs, all of the girls cheered "Yaaaay, its Debra." And that made Debra feel great.

Debra didn't have any idea what happened at the Fairmont Elementary School Cool Girls Club, but she soon found out.

4

The girls ate from big bowls of pretzels and potato chips. They talked about school and complained about their little brothers and sisters.

Darlene and Bethany played card games, and Grace and Annie played with Maggie's dolls. Debra played catch with Heather.

Then Maggie announced, "It's time for our club initiation! Debra, step forward."

All of a sudden all of the girls stopped what they were doing and stood near Maggie. Debra was a little confused and a little worried.

"What's an initiation?" Debra asked. She didn't think she even liked the sound of the word.

"It's what clubs do with new members," Maggie replied. "To prove that you deserve to be in the Cool Girls Club, you have to do something cool."

Maggie went behind the couch and came back with a brown bottle.

Maggie held it out to Debra and said, "All new members have to drink a bottle of beer! Then we'll know that you're cool enough to belong to the club."

Debra didn't know what to do.

"Kids aren't supposed to drink beer!" she thought to herself.

Debra wondered if this was some kind of joke. Maybe Maggie had put water in the beer bottle and it was just a test!

"But what if it really is beer?" Debra said to herself. "Beer doesn't taste good, and it might make me sick. What would my parents say?"

Many thoughts were racing through Debra's head as Maggie took a bottle opener and popped the metal cap off the beer.

"She's not kidding…" Debra thought to herself, what should I do?"

But just then Maggie's mother shouted down from the kitchen. "Debra, your mother is here to pick you up!"

Debra ran up the stairs as quickly as she could. She turned around at the top of the stairs and said: "Bye. See you at school." She saw that Maggie must have put away the beer, because she waved both her hands to say goodbye.

"We'll continue the initiation at the next meeting!" Maggie called after Debra. "We'll have the next meeting at your house!"

For the entire week Debra couldn't think of anything but the Cool Girls Club and Maggie's promise to continue the initiation.

On Wednesday, Heather came home with Debra to work on their class science project. They were making a clay model of a brain.

Debra thought that this would be a good time to find out more about the initiation, and she asked Heather, "Did you have to drink beer when you first joined the Club?"

"Of course," Heather said. "We all did. That's how we know if you're cool or not. Beer tastes funny and it makes you feel kind of dizzy, but you get used to it. My big sister drinks beer all of the time, and she lets me sneak a sip sometimes."

Then Heather added, "But don't tell your parents or anyone else. That definitely wouldn't be cool."

The days went quickly, and all too soon it was Saturday morning, the day of the Cool Girls Club Meeting at Debra's house. It was also the day that Maggie and the other girls would expect her to drink beer.

Debra thought to herself, "I know that drinking beer is wrong, but I want to be in the Club. I bet they kicked out Katie because she wouldn't drink any beer. I guess they'll kick me out, too!

"But maybe it isn't so bad to drink just a little bit of beer," She thought, "I don't even know why beer is so bad!"

Debra decided to ask her mother why it was wrong to drink beer.

Debra went down to the kitchen where her mother was setting the table for breakfast.

"Mom," Debra began, "why is it wrong for kids to drink beer?"

Debra's mother stopped for a second and turned to her daughter. She wondered why Debra was asking that question at eight am on a Saturday morning, and she wondered if something was wrong. But she knew that Debra would tell her if something was really bothering her.

It's always a good idea to ask a grown-up if you are confused about something. I asked my Mom and Dad about why you shouldn't eat a worm on the end of a fish hook. I'm glad I asked!

Debra's mom explained, "Beer and wine and liquor contain a chemical called alcohol that can make children feel bad and get sick. As you know, some grown-ups drink beer or wine or other drinks with alcohol, but their brains and bodies are different than children. A little bit of alcohol won't hurt them."

"But if adults drink too much alcohol, they will be sick too. If they drink a lot of drinks with alcohol every day, they will have a serious problem with their health. Drinks with alcohol also make your thinking fuzzy, like when you are very, very tired and you can't think clearly. That's why adults should never drink and drive. Their thinking is not clear, and they could get in a bad accident and even kill somebody."

"Drinking beer and wine is a big problem for a lot of people and that's another reason why you have to be grown-up to try it."

Debra wasn't sure she understood everything that her mother had told her about beer and the other stuff with alcohol in it. But she was sure that her mother knew what was best.

Debra knew that it was important to follow adult rules. She thought: "Adults have lived a lot longer than kids, and that's why they know the right things to do."

Debra loved her mom and dad and she knew they loved her, too. She knew that they wouldn't tell her something that was wrong.

It's nice to be loved. I love Debra, too.

31

At exactly three o'clock the door bell rang, and Annie, Grace and Maggie came in. Five minutes later Darlene, Bethany and Heather rang the door. Debra's mother said that the girls could play outside or go to the family room and play.

Maggie said, "We'll go up to the family room for our meeting." Maggie was carrying a big backpack, and Debra thought she heard something in the pack go "clink" while Maggie was closing the door of the family room.

"Is that the beer?" Debra thought to herself.

"Well," said Maggie, "I guess now that we're all here it is time to continue the initiation!"

Maggie reached into her backpack and pulled out the same brown bottle that Debra had seen the week before and a bottle opener. Then she brought out two more bottles of beer.

"Debra, you're going to drink the first bottle all by yourself," Maggie said, "that's what every new member of the Cool Girls Club has to do. Then the rest of us will drink these other two bottles of beer."

Maggie opened the first bottle and held it out to Debra.

"No, thank you." Debra said politely. "I don't want any beer, and I don't think you should have it either."

Maggie didn't seem that surprised that Debra didn't want to take the beer.

"Don't be afraid," she said to Debra in a sweet calm voice, "it won't taste that bad. After you drink a little you won't even taste it. You can hold your nose if you like."

"No, thank you," Debra said again, this time with a little more firmness in your voice. "Children shouldn't drink anything with alcohol in it. That's the rule, and that's what I believe."

Maggie continued to hold out the beer. She didn't seem surprised that Debra was refusing to take the beer.

"I think that you're just afraid to drink the beer," Maggie said, staring Debra straight in the eye. "I dare you to take it and if you don't, you're just a little baby."

"Yeah, we dare you," said Heather.

"We dare you," said Grace.

"We double dare you," said Bethany and she put her hands on her hips and gave Debra a mean look.

"When I say 'no,' I mean 'no,'" said Debra, now with anger in her voice. And she put her hands on her hips and stared right back at Bethany.

"Now why don't you put your stupid beer back in your backpack and come with me outside. We can play on my swing set or do something that is fun."

And with that, Debra opened the door and walked out of the room.

"You're a chicken!" Grace said.

"You're a baby!" Bethany said.

"You're going to be kicked out of the
Cool Girls Club!" Maggie said.

But Debra just kept walking away.

45

Debra walked by the kitchen, waved to her mom, and went outside. Heather and Bethany were right behind her and then Grace, Annie, and Darlene went outside too. Maggie was the last to come outside. She looked mad.

Debra jumped on a swing, stomach first, and went high in the air. Grace jumped on the other swing stomach first, too. It was a bright sunny day and the other girls were soon climbing on the monkey bars and taking turns pushing each other on the swings.

Maggie decided to sit down on her backpack and just watch. She glared at Debra and would sometimes give a dirty look to one of the other girls. But no one paid her much attention.

On Monday Debra went back to school. When she opened her locker, she noticed a note on the locker floor that someone had slipped in.

It said: "YOU'RE OUT OF THE CLUB!"

"Big deal," Debra thought to herself. "They think that they have a Cool Girls Club, but I think they have a Fool Girls Club."

At recess Debra saw all of the girls in the club, and she was surprised that they were all nice to her, except for Maggie, who stayed as far away from Debra as possible. Debra even played dodge ball with Bethany and Heather and Darlene, and it was as if nothing had ever happened.

As she was going back to her classroom, Debra thought to herself, "Maybe I'll start my own club and just invite girls who want to do fun things and not things that are dangerous or wrong. Our initiation would be to bake cookies or brownies to share. That's the kind of initiation I'd like!"

51

1. Talk to a grown-up about what is right and wrong.

2. Believe in yourself and what you think is right.

3. Stand up for your rights, no matter what anyone says to you.

4. Don't let the desire to be popular change your decisions.

5. Find friends whom you can have fun with and who enjoy the things that you like to do.

FLORIDA

Teaching Children
To Deal With Peer Pressure

Peer pressure is a powerful force in the lives of children. I'm sure that you remember when you were a child how much pressure there was on you to wear the right clothes, to use the latest slang, and be to liked by the right kids. There were also probably times that other kids made you feel you should do something that you knew was wrong, like drinking alcohol, smoking cigarettes, lying or even stealing. Children are faced with moral and values-oriented decisions every day, and you can help them learn to make the right choices.

Unfortunately, many adults feel that when children enter elementary school there isn't much that they can do about helping them with their social problems. But that simply isn't true. Children and even teenagers look to adults for guidance when they are faced with difficult issues. Children benefit from adult advice, from conversations about their feelings, and in particular from role-playing situations where children can practice what to say in the real-life problems. If you know a child that is having a hard time with his or her peers, take the time to talk about these situations. Reading this book and talking about how Debra handles peer pressure will be a good start. Children need 10 or 15 minutes a day, every day, to help them in their emotional development. When you take this time, you can make a profound difference in the lives of the children that you care about.

54

Other Great Books from the Emotional Literacy Series

To place an order or to get a catalog,
please write, call, or visit our web-site.

CTC Publishing
A Division of Courage To Change
10400 Eaton Place, Suite 140
Fairfax, Virginia 22030
1-800-942-0962
www.couragetochange.com

The Emotional Literacy Series

This new book series helps children understand their emotions and behaviors with friendly advice from Dr. Larry and a gang of amusing cartoon characters. Each book explores a particular topic — anger, teasing, excess energy, childhood obesity and peer pressure — from the point of view of the child, and offers child-friendly advice on how to deal with the problem. Each book begins with a letter to the boys and girls reading the book from the author, Dr. Larry Shapiro. Dr. Larry introduces the subject in a reassuring, non-judgmental tone and tells kids: "All feelings are okay. It's what you do with them that counts!"

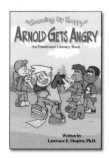

Arnold Gets Angry

Everyone gets angry sometimes. In this appealing book, Arnold and his friends learn about what makes them angry...and how to control their anger by talking about it to friends, parents, teachers. The book is child-friendly and fun to read as it teaches problem-solving skills that really work! ISBN: 0-9747789-0-7

67312   Arnold Gets Angry..................................**$17.95**

Betty Stops the Bully

Nobody likes to be bullied or teased. And many children, like Betty, don't know how to make it stop. This story suggests sensible things to do when confronted by a bully. It also helps children who are bullies learn new social skills. ISBN: 0-9747789-1-5

67313 Betty Stops the Bully.........................$17.95

Catherine Finds Her Courage

All kids are scared sometimes. Fear is a normal part of life. But some children have fears that impede their learning and making friends. This book helps children recognize some of the most common fears of childhood. ISBN: 0-9747789-2-3

67314 Catherine Finds Her Courage $17.95

Freddie Fights Fat

Being overweight is a problem for a lot of kids. Freddy didn't think he was chubby, until he noticed his clothes were too tight and he couldn't keep up with the other kids in sports. This story teaches children how to change bad eating habits and lose weight by eating healthier foods, exercising, and spending less time in front of the TV. ISBN: 0-9747789-5-8

67873 Freddie Fights Fat $17.95

Ethan Has Too Much Energy

Some kids have too much energy all of the time. They don't do well in school even though they are smart. And adults are often punishing them for misbehavior even when they are trying to behave well. This book teaches a variety of self-control techniques that help Ethan and all young children act more responsibly and do better at school and at home.

67317 Ethan Has Too Much Energy $17.95

Hey, Dad — Let's Learn!
Early Learning Activity Cards

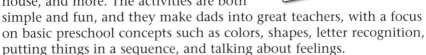

Designed to strengthen the ties between fathers and their young children, the ninety cards in this deck provide ninety imaginative learning activities that take just a few minutes each to do.

Dads and their kids make music with rubber bands, do silly dances, take nature walks, make shaving-cream mustaches, look for circles around the house, and more. The activities are both simple and fun, and they make dads into great teachers, with a focus on basic preschool concepts such as colors, shapes, letter recognition, putting things in a sequence, and talking about feelings.

68018   *Hey Dad, Let's Learn!* $15.95

Hi, Dad, Let's Write!
A postcard set for dads and kids

These cards were designed to help dads play an important role in their children's lives even though they may be far apart. (Moms can use them too!) The set contains two packs of 25 postcards, one for dads to send to their kids and one for kids to send to their dads.

Each postcard is preprinted with a "thought starter" to help the writer get started: *"I'll tell you something funny that happened ..."* or *"If you were here right now we'd ..."* or *"You won't believe what happened in school today ..."*, for example.

When it's not possible for fathers to be with their children, sending frequent messages openly expressing thoughts and feelings can make a tremendous difference in developing a positive relationship.

68070   Hi Dad — Let's Write postcard set $17.95

ORDER FORM

CTC·PUBLISHING
10400 Eaton Place, Suite 140
Fairfax, Virginia 22030

For Credit Card Orders,

 *Fax This Order Form To:*

1-800-772-6499

OR

 Call Toll-Free:

1-800-942-0962

Sold to: (Please Print)

Order Code (Above Name on Mailing Label) _____

Name _____

Company _____

Address _____

City _____ State _____ Zip _____

Ship to: (Only if different from "Sold to.")

Name _____

Company _____

Address _____

City _____ State _____ Zip _____

Your Credit Card Number

Expiration Date

X _____
Signature (as shown on credit card)

Telephone:

Daytime:
(_____)_____

Evening:
(_____)_____

E-mail:
_____

Method of Payment

☐ **Check or Money Order Enclosed**
(payable to Courage To Change)

☐ **VISA** ☐ **MasterCard**

☐ **American Express Card** ☐ **DISCOVER**

THANK YOU FOR YOUR ORDER!

Item #	Qty	Title or Description	Price Ea.	Total

Attach additional sheets if necessary

	Subtotal	

Shipping & Handling
(to each delivery address)

Add: US Shipping, Handling & Ins.

Merchandise Total:	Add:
Under $25	$ 8.95
$26 - $50	$ 9.95
$51 - $75	$ 10.95
$76 - $100	$ 12.95
$101 - $125	$ 13.95
$126 - $150	$ 14.95
Over $150	$ 15.95

TOTAL

Residents of VA add 5% Sales Tax

Total